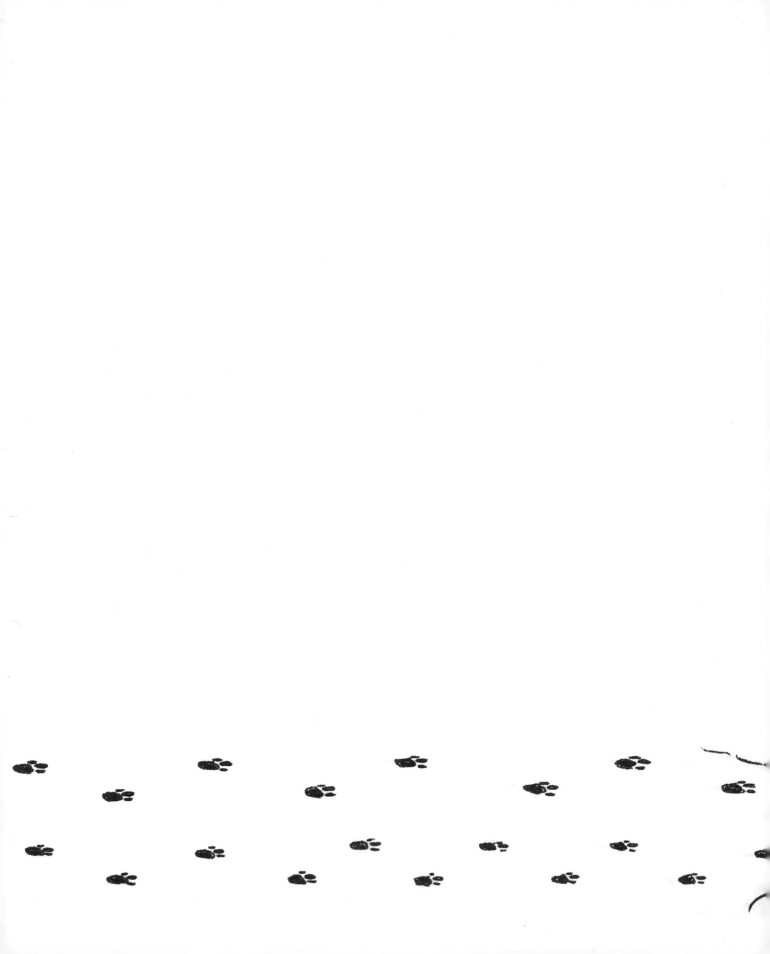

PILLOW KEEPS MOVING!

by Laura Gehl   illustrated by Christopher Weyant

VIKING

Then your footstool is not broken, sir.
Would you like a pin?

For Kevin, whose tremendous heart
brightens our lives every day.
—L.G.

For Anna, Kate, and Lily, who love all animals,
especially their dog, Hudson, who loves them back.
—C.W.

VIKING
Penguin Young Readers
An imprint of Penguin Random House LLC
375 Hudson Street
New York, New York 10014

First published in the United States of America by Viking,
an imprint of Penguin Random House LLC, 2018

Text copyright © 2018 by Laura Gehl
Illustrations copyright © 2018 by Christopher Weyant

LIBRARY OF CONGRESS CATALOGING-IN-PUBLICATION DATA
Names: Gehl, Laura, author. | Weyant, Christopher, illustrator.
Title: My pillow keeps moving! / written by Laura Gehl ; illustrated by Christopher Weyant.
Description: New York : Viking, [2018] | Audience: Ages 4-8. | Summary: "A clever pup ends up in a cozy home,
and she'll do anything to stay there. She impersonates everything the lonely homeowner needs—
a pillow, a footstool, a jacket. But in the end, being herself works best"—Provided by publisher.
Identifiers: LCCN 2017033429 | ISBN 9780425288245 (hardcover) Subjects: | CYAC: Dog adoption—Fiction. | Stores, Retail—Fiction. |
Loneliness—Fiction. | Humorous stories. | BISAC: JUVENILE FICTION / Animals / Dogs. | JUVENILE FICTION / Family / General (see also
headings under Social Issues). | JUVENILE FICTION / Humorous Stories. Classification: LCC PZ7.G2588 My 2018 | DDC [E]—dc23
LC record available at https://lccn.loc.gov/2017033429

Printed in China   Set in Burbank Big

1 2 3 4 5 6 7 8 9 10

The illustrations were created on Arches paper with watercolor and ink and a smidgen of digital magic.